# Pat the Cat

## Colin and
## Jacqui Hawkins

**DK**

**DORLING KINDERSLEY**
London • New York • Stuttgart

# Do you know Pat the cat?

A DORLING KINDERSLEY BOOK

Published in the United Kingdom in 1995
by Dorling Kindersley Limited,
9 Henrietta Street, London WC2E 8PS

Published in the United States in 1995
by Dorling Kindersley Publishing, Inc.,
95 Madison Avenue, New York, New York 10016

2 4 6 8 10 9 7 5 3

ISBN 0-7513-5352-3 (UK)
ISBN 0-7894-0154-1 (US)

Reproduction by DOT Gradations
Printed in Italy by L.E.G.O.

# He's very fat.

f

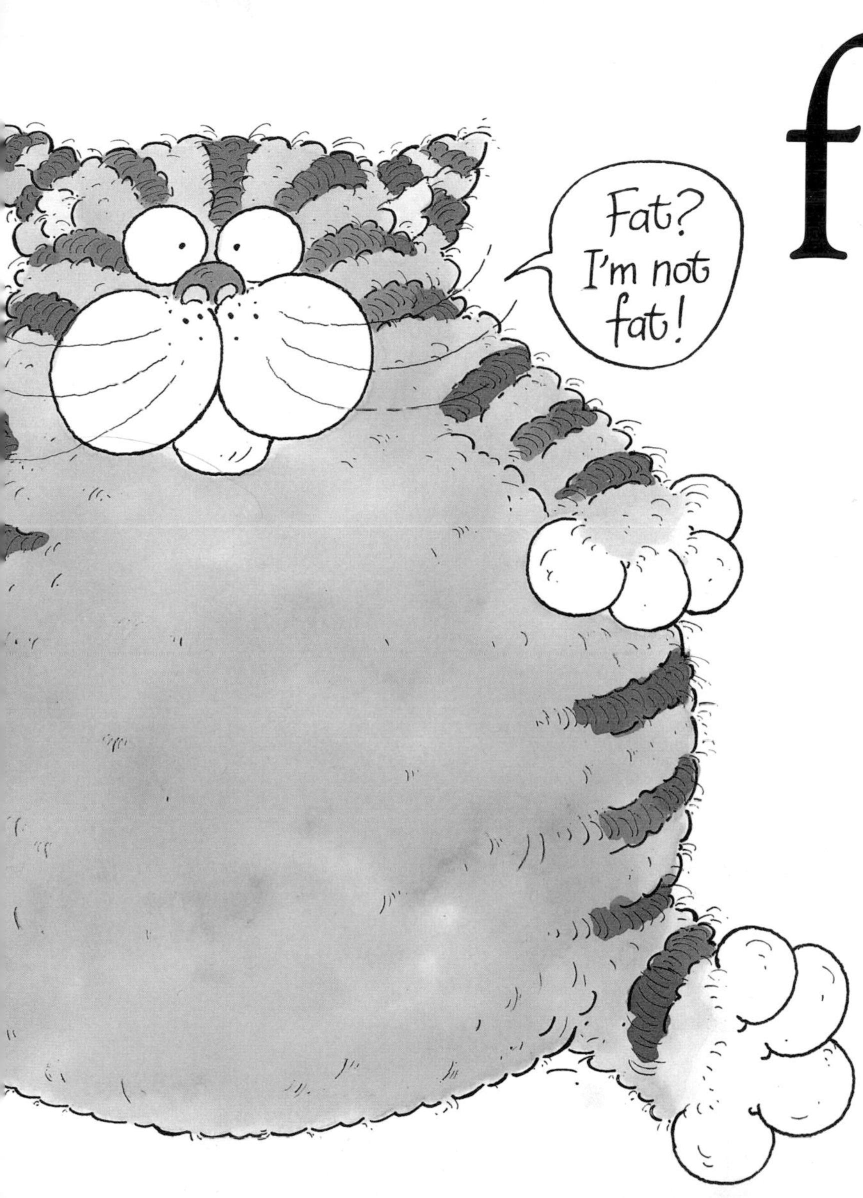

He wears a top hat
when he sits on his mat.

But look! Who's that in
Pat's hat?

# It's Tat the bat

and Nat the rat.

Pat is too fat to get Nat out of his hat.

# So that's where he sat.

S

While Pat sat, out
popped Nat.

Now there's a hole in the hat of the cat called Pat.